THE
GOLD
OF
THE
TIGERS

JORGE LUIS BORGES

THE GOLD OF THE TIGERS

Selected later poems

Translated by
Alastair Reid

A Bilingual Edition

E. P. Dutton   New York

Library of Congress Cataloging in Publication Data
Borges, Jorge Luis, 1899–
    The gold of the tigers.
    Selections, with English translations, from the author's El oro de los tigres and La rosa profunda.
    I. Reid, Alastair. II. Borges, Jorge Luis, 1899–
La rosa profunda. English & Spanish. Selections. 1977. III. Title.
PQ7797.B63507413 1977   861   77–7479

Parts of this book have appeared in the following publications:
The New Yorker: "The Watcher," "The Palace," "Hengist Wants Men, A.D. 449," "Brunanburh, A.D. 937," "To the Nightingale," "Talismans"
The New York Review of Books: "The Blind Man," "A Blind Man," "Browning Resolves To Be a Poet," "To the German Language"
Translation: "The Gold of the Tigers," "The Unending Rose"
American Poetry Review: "You," "Inventory," "I Am," "My Books"
New Republic: "Tankas," "Fifteen Coins," "Elegy," "Milonga of Manuel Flores," "I," "Poem of Quantity," "Susana Bombal"

ISBN: 0-525-11458-0 (cloth)
        0-525-03465-X (paper)

Published simultaneously in Canada by Clarke, Irwin & Company Limited, Toronto and Vancouver

10 9 8 7 6 5 4 3 2 1

First Edition

CONTENTS

For anyone who has lived out seventy years, according to the Book of David, there is little to hope for except to go on plying familiar skills, with an occasional mild variation and with tedious repetitions. To escape, or possibly to extenuate, that monotony, I chose to admit, perhaps with rash hospitality, the miscellaneous interests that crossed my everyday writer's attention. Parable follows on the heels of confession, free or blank verse on the sonnet. In the earliest times, which were so susceptible to vague speculation and the inevitable ordering of the universe, there can have existed no division between the poetic and the prosaic. Everything must have been tinged with magic. Thor was not the god of thunder; he was the thunder and the god.

For a true poet, every moment of existence, every act, ought to be poetic since, in essence, it is so. As far as I know, no one to this day has attained that high state of awareness. Browning and Blake got closer to it than anyone else. Whitman aimed in that direction, but his careful enumerations do not always rise above a kind of crude cataloguing.

I distrust literary schools, which I judge to be didactic constructs designed to simplify what they preach; but if I were obliged to name the influence behind my poems, I would say they stemmed from *modernismo*—that enormous liberation that gave new life to the many literatures that use the Castilian language, and that certainly carried as far as Spain. I have spoken more than once with Leopoldo Lugones—that solitary, proud man—and he would interrupt the flow of the conversation to mention "my friend and master, Rubén Darío." (I think, furthermore, that we ought to emphasize the affinities

7

within our language, and not its regional differences.)

My reader will notice, in some pages, a philosophical preoccupation. It has been with me since my childhood, when my father showed me, with the help of a chess-board (it was, I remember, a cedarwood board), the paradox of the race between Achilles and the tortoise.

As for the influences that show up in this volume . . . First, the writers I prefer—I have already mentioned Robert Browning; next, those I have read and whom I echo; then, those I have never read but who are in me. A language is a tradition, a way of grasping reality, not an arbitrary assemblage of symbols.

JORGE LUIS BORGES

Buenos Aires, 1972

The romantic notion of a Muse who inspires poets was advanced by classical writers; the classical idea of the poem as a function of the intelligence was put forward by a romantic, Poe, around 1846. The fact is paradoxical. Apart from isolated cases of oneiric inspiration—the shepherd's dream referred to by Bede, the famous dream of Coleridge—it is obvious that both doctrines are partially true, unless they correspond to distinct stages in the process. (For Muse, we must read what the Hebrews and Milton called Spirit, and what our own woeful mythology refers to as the Subconscious.) In my own case, the process is more or less unvarying. I begin with the glimpse of a form, a kind of remote island, which will eventually be a story or a poem. I see the end and I see the beginning, but not what is in between. That is gradually revealed to me, when the stars or chance are propitious. More than once, I have to retrace my steps by way of the shadows. I try to interfere as little as possible in the evolution of the work. I do not want it to be distorted by my opinions, which are the most trivial things about us. The notion of art as compromise is a simplification, for no one knows entirely what he is doing. A writer can conceive a fable, Kipling acknowledged, without grasping its moral. He must be true to his imagination, and not to the mere ephemeral circumstances of a supposed "reality."

Literature starts out from poetry and can take centuries to arrive at the possibility of prose. After four hundred years, the Anglo-Saxons left behind a poetry which was not just occasionally admirable and a prose which was scarcely explicit. The word must have been in the beginning a magic symbol, which the usury of time wore out. The mission of the poet should be to restore to the word, at least in a partial way, its primitive and now secret force. All verse should have two obligations: to communicate a precise instance and to touch us physically, as the presence of the sea does. I have here an example from Virgil:

sunt lacrymae rerum et mentem mortalia tangunt

One from Meredith:

Not till the fire is dying in the grate
Look we for any kinship with the stars

Or this alexandrine from Lugones, in which the Spanish is trying to return to the Latin:

El hombre numeroso de penas y de días.

Such verses move along their shifting path in the memory.

After so many—too many—years of practicing literature, I do not profess any aesthetic. Why add to the natural limits which habit imposes on us those of some theory or other? Theories, like convictions of a political or religious nature, are nothing more than stimuli. They vary for every writer. Whitman was right to do away with rhyme; that negation would have been stupid in Victor Hugo's case.

Going over the proofs of this book, I notice with some distaste that blindness plays a mournful role, which it does not play in my life. Blindness is a confinement, but it is also a liberation, a solitude propitious to invention, a key and an algebra.

JORGE LUIS BORGES

June, 1975

THE
GOLD
OF
THE
TIGERS

TANKAS

1

Alto en la cumbre
todo el jardín es luna,
luna de oro.
Más precioso es el roce
de tu boca en la sombra.

2

La voz del ave
que la penumbra esconde
ha enmudecido.
Andas por tu jardín.
Algo, lo sé, te falta.

3

La ajena copa,
la espada que fue espada
en otra mano,
la luna de la calle,
¿dime, acaso no bastan?

4

Bajo la luna
el tigre de oro y sombra
mira sus garras.
No sabe que en el alba
han destrozado un hombre.

TANKAS

1

High on the summit,
the garden is all moonlight,
the moon is golden.
More precious is the contact
of your lips in the shadow.

2

The sound of a bird
which the twilight is hiding
has fallen silent.
You pace the garden.
I know that you miss something.

3

The curious goblet,
the sword which was a sword once
in another grasp,
the moonlight on the street—
tell me, are they not enough?

4

Underneath the moon,
tiger of gold and shadow
looks down at his claws,
unaware that in the dawn
they lacerated a man.

5

Triste la lluvia
que sobre el mármol cae,
triste ser tierra.
Triste no ser los días
del hombre, el sueño, el alba.

6

No haber caído,
como otros de mi sangre,
en la batalla.
Ser en la vana noche
él que cuenta las sílabas.

5

Wistful is the rain
falling upon the marble,
sad to become earth,
sad no longer to be part
of man, of dream, of morning.

6

Not to have fallen,
like others of my lineage,
cut down in battle.
To be in the fruitless night
he who counts the syllables.

SUSANA BOMBAL

Alta en la tarde, altiva y alabada,
cruza el casto jardín y está en la exacta
luz del instante irreversible y puro
que nos da este jardín y la alta imagen
silenciosa. La veo aquí y ahora,
pero también la veo en un antiguo
crepúsculo de Ur de los Caldeos
o descendiendo por las lentas gradas
de un templo, que es innumerable polvo
del planeta y que fue piedra y soberbia,
o descifrando el mágico alfabeto
de las estrellas de otras latitudes
o aspirando una rosa en Inglaterra.
Está donde haya música, en el leve
azul, en el hexámetro del griego,
en nuestras soledades que la buscan,
en el espejo de agua de la fuente,
en el mármol de tiempo, en una espada,
en la serenidad de una terraza
que divisa ponientes y jardines.

Y detrás de los mitos y las máscaras,
el alma, que está sola.

SUSANA BOMBAL

Tall in the evening, arrogant, aloof,
she crosses the chaste garden and is caught
in the shutter of that pure and fleeting instant
which gives to us this garden and this vision,
unspeaking, deep. I see her here and now,
but simultaneously I also see her
haunting an ancient, twilit Ur of the Chaldees
or coming slowly down the shallow steps,
a temple, which was once proud stone but now
has turned to an infinity of dust,
or winkling out the magic alphabet
locked in the stars of other latitudes,
or breathing in a rose's scent, in England.
She is where music is, and in the gentle
blue of the sky, in Greek hexameters,
and in our solitudes, which seek her out.
She is mirrored in the water of the fountain,
in time's memorial marble, in a sword,
in the serene air of a patio,
looking out on sunsets and on gardens.

And underneath the myths and the masks,
her soul, always alone.

COSAS

El volumen caído que los otros
ocultan en la hondura del estante
y que los días y las noches cubren
de lento polvo silencioso. El ancla
de sidón que los mares de Inglaterra
oprimen en su abismo ciego y blando.
El espejo que no repite a nadie
cuando la casa se ha quedado sola.
Las limaduras de uña que dejamos
a lo largo del tiempo y del espacio.
El polvo indescifrable que fue Shakespeare.
Las modificaciones de la nube.
La simétrica rosa momentánea
que el azar dio una vez a los ocultos
cristales del pueril calidoscopio.
Los remos de Argos, la primera nave.
Las pisadas de arena que la ola
soñolienta y fatal borra en la playa.
Los colores de Turner cuando apagan
las luces en la recta galería
y no resuena un paso en la alta noche.
El revés del prolijo mapamundi.
La tenue telaraña en la pirámide.
La piedra ciega y la curiosa mano.
El sueño que he tenido antes del alba
y que olvidé cuando clareaba el día.
El principio y el fin de la epopeya
de Finsburh, hoy unos contados versos
de hierro, no gastado por los siglos.
La letra inversa en el papel secante.
La tortuga en el fondo del aljibe.
Lo que no puede ser. El otro cuerno

THINGS

The fallen volume, hidden by the others
from sight in the recesses of the bookshelves,
and which the days and nights muffle over
with slow and noiseless dust. Also, the anchor
of Sidon, which the seas surrounding England
press down into its blind and soft abyss.
The mirror which shows nobody's reflection
after the house has long been left alone.
Fingernail filings which we leave behind
across the long expanse of time and space.
The indecipherable dust, once Shakespeare.
The changing figurations of a cloud.
The momentary but symmetric rose
which once, by chance, took substance in the shrouded
mirrors of a boy's kaleidoscope.
The oars of Argus, the original ship.
The sandy footprints which the fatal wave
as though asleep erases from the beach.
The colors of a Turner when the lights
are turned out in the narrow gallery
and not a footstep sounds in the deep night.
The other side of the dreary map of the world.
The tenuous spiderweb in the pyramid.
The sightless stone and the inquiring hand.
The dream I had in the approaching dawn
and later lost in the clearing of the day.
The ending and beginning of the epic
of Finsburh, today a few sparse verses
of iron, unwasted by the centuries.
The mirrored letter on the blotting paper.
The turtle in the bottom of the cistern.
And that which cannot be. The other horn

del unicornio. El Ser que es Tres y es Uno.
El disco triangular. El inasible
instante en que la flecha del eleata,
inmóvil en el aire, da en el blanco.
La flor entre las páginas de Becquer.
El péndulo que el tiempo ha detenido.
El acero que Odín clavó en el árbol.
El texto de las no cortadas hojas.
El eco de los cascos de la carga
de Junín, que de algún eterno modo
no ha cesado y es parte de la trama.
La sombra de Sarmiento en las aceras.
La voz que oyó el pastor en la montaña.
La osamenta blanqueando en el desierto.
La bala que mató a Francisco Borges.
El otro lado del tapiz. Las cosas
que nadie mira, salvo el Dios de Berkeley.

of the unicorn. The Being, Three in One.
The triangular disc. The imperceptible moment
in which the Eleatic arrow,
motionless in the air, reaches the mark.
The violet pressed between the leaves of Becquer.
The pendulum which time has stayed in place.
The weapon Odin buried in the tree.
The volume with its pages still unslit.
The echo of the hoofbeats at the charge
of Junin, which in some enduring mode
never has ceased, is part of the webbed scheme.
The shadow of Sarmiento on the sidewalks.
The voice heard by the shepherd on the mountain.
The skeleton bleaching white in the desert.
The bullet which shot dead Francisco Borges.
The other side of the tapestry. The things
which no one sees, except for Berkeley's God.

EL AMENAZADO

Es el amor. Tendré que ocultarme o que huir.

Crecen los muros de su cárcel, como en un sueño atroz.

La hermosa máscara ha cambiado, pero como siempre es la única. ¿De qué me servirán mis talismanes: el ejercicio de las letras, la vaga erudición, el aprendizaje de las palabras que usó el áspero Norte para cantar sus mares y sus espadas, la serena amistad, las galerías de la Biblioteca, las cosas comunes, los hábitos, el joven amor de mi madre, la sombra militar de mis muertos, la noche intemporal, el sabor del sueño?

Estar contigo o no estar contigo es la medida de mi tiempo.

Ya el cántaro se quiebra sobre la fuente, ya el hombre se levanta a la voz del ave, ya se han oscurecido los que miran por las ventanas, pero la sombra no ha traído la paz.

Es, ya lo sé, el amor: la ansieded y el alivio de oír tu voz, la espera y la memoria, el horror de vivir en lo sucesivo.

Es el amor con sus mitologías, con sus pequeñas magias inútiles.

Hay una esquina por la que no me atrevo a pasar.

Ya los ejércitos me cercan, las hordas.

(Esta habitación es irreal; ella no la ha visto.)

El nombre de una mujer me delata.

Me duele una mujer en todo el cuerpo.

THE THREATENED ONE

It is love. I will have to hide or flee.

Its prison walls grow larger, as in a fearful dream. The alluring mask has changed, but as usual it is the only one. What use now are my talismans, my touchstones: the practice of literature, vague learning, an apprenticeship to the language used by the flinty Northland to sing of its seas and its swords, the serenity of friendship, the galleries of the Library, ordinary things, habits, the young love of my mother, the soldierly shadow cast by my dead ancestors, the timeless night, the flavor of sleep and dream?

Being with you or without you is how I measure my time.

Now the water jug shatters above the spring, now the man rises to the sound of birds, now those who look through the windows are indistinguishable, but the darkness has not brought peace.

It is love, I know it; the anxiety and relief at hearing your voice, the hope and the memory, the horror at living in succession.

It is love with its own mythology, its minor and pointless magic.

There is a street corner I do not dare to pass.

Now the armies surround me, the rabble.

(This room is unreal. She has not seen it.)

A woman's name has me in thrall.

A woman's being afflicts my whole body.

TÚ

Un solo hombre ha nacido, un solo hombre ha muerto en
    la tierra.
Afirmar lo contrario es mera estadística, es una adición
    imposible.
No menos imposible que sumar el olor de la lluvia y el
    sueño que antenoche soñaste.
Ese hombre es Ulises, Abel, Caín, el primer hombre que
    ordenó las constelaciones, el hombre que erigió la
    primer pirámide, el hombre que escribió los hexa-
    gramas del Libro de los Cambios, el forjador que
    grabó runas en la espada de Hengist, el arquero
    Einar Tamberskelver, Luis de León, el librero que
    engendró a Samuel Johnson, el jardinero de Vol-
    taire, Darwin en la proa del *Beagle,* un judío en la
    cámara letal, con el tiempo, tú y yo.
Un solo hombre ha muerto en Ilión, en el Metauro, en
    Hastings, en Austerlitz, en Trafalgar, en Gettysburg.
Un solo hombre ha muerto en los hospitales, en barcos,
    en la ardua soledad, en la alcoba del hábito y del
    amor.
Un solo hombre ha mirado la vasta aurora.
Un solo hombre ha sentido en el paladar la frescura del
    agua, el sabor de las frutas y de la carne.
Hablo del único, del uno, del que siempre está solo.

YOU

In all the world, one man has been born, one man has
    died.
To insist otherwise is nothing more than statistics, an
    impossible extension.
No less impossible than bracketing the smell of rain with
    your dream of two nights ago.
That man is Ulysses, Abel, Cain, the first to make con-
    stellations of the stars, to build the first pyramid,
    the man who contrived the hexagrams of the Book
    of Changes, the smith who engraved runes on the
    sword of Hengist, Einar Tamberskelver the archer,
    Luis de León, the bookseller who fathered Samuel
    Johnson, Voltaire's gardener, Darwin aboard the
    Beagle, a Jew in the death chamber, and, in time,
    you and I.
One man alone has died at Troy, at Metaurus, at Hast-
    ings, at Austerlitz, at Trafalgar, at Gettysburg.
One man alone has died in hospitals, in boats, in painful
    solitude, in the rooms of habit and of love.
One man alone has looked on the enormity of dawn.
One man alone has felt on his tongue the fresh quench-
    ing of water, the flavor of fruit and of flesh.
I speak of the unique, the single man, he who is always
    alone.

POEMA DE LA CANTIDAD

Pienso en el parco cielo puritano
de solitarias y perdidas luces
que Emerson miraría tantas noches
desde la nieve y el rigor de Concord.
Aquí son demasiadas las estrellas.
El hombre es demasiado. Las innúmeras
generaciones de aves y de insectos,
del jaguar constelado y de la sierpe,
de ramas que se tejen y entretejen,
del café, de la arena y de las hojas
oprimen las mañanas y prodigan
su minucioso laberinto inútil.
Acaso cada hormiga que pisamos
es única ante Dios, que la precisa
para la ejecución de las puntuales
leyes que rigen Su curioso mundo.
Si así no fuera, el universo entero
sería un error y un oneroso caos.
Los espejos del ébano y del agua,
el espejo inventivo de los sueños,
los líquenes, los peces, las madréporas,
las filas de tortugas en el tiempo,
las luciérnagas de una sola tarde,
las dinastías de las araucarias,
las perfiladas letras de un volumen
que la noche no borra, son sin duda
no menos personales y enigmáticas
que yo, que las confundo. No me atrevo
a juzgar a la lepra o a Calígula.

POEM OF QUANTITY

I think of the stark and puritanical sky
with its remote and solitary stars
which Emerson so many nights would look at
from the snow-bound severity of Concord.
Here, the night sky overflows with stars.
Man is too numerous. Endless generations
of birds and insects, multiplying themselves,
of serpents and the spotted jaguar,
of growing branches, weaving, interweaving,
of grains of sand, of coffee and of leaves
descend on every day and recreate
their minuscule and useless labyrinth.
It may be every ant we trample on
is single before God, Who counts on it
for the unfolding of the measured laws
which regulate His curious universe.
The entire system, if it was not so,
would be an error and a weighty chaos.
Mirrors of water, mirrors of ebony,
the all-inventive mirror of our dreams,
lichens, fishes, and the riddled coral,
the clawmarks left by tortoises in time,
the fireflies of a single afternoon,
the dynasties of the Auraucarians,
the delicate shapes of letters in a volume
which night does not blot out, unquestionably
are no less personal and enigmatic
than I, who mix them up. I would not venture
to judge the lepers or Caligula.

EL CENTINELA

Entra la luz y me recuerdo; ahí está.

Empieza por decirme su nombre, que es (ya se entiende) el mío.

Vuelvo a la esclavitud que ha durado más de siete veces diez años.

Me impone su memoria.

Me impone las miserias de cada día, la condición humana.

Soy su viejo enfermero; me obliga a que le lave los pies.

Me acecha en los espejos, en la caoba, en los cristales de las tiendas.

Una u otra mujer lo han rechazado y debo compartir su congoja.

Me dicta ahora este poema, que no me gusta.

Me exige el nebuloso aprendizaje del terco anglosajón.

Me ha convertido al culto idolátrico de militares muertos, con los que acaso no podría cambiar una sola palabra.

En el último tramo de la escalera siento que está a mi lado.

Está en mis pasos, en mi voz.

Minuciosamente lo odio.

Advierto con fruición que casi no ve.

Estoy en una celda circular y el infinito muro se estrecha.

Ninguno de los dos engaña al otro, pero los dos mentimos.

Nos conocemos demasiado, inseparable hermano.

Bebes el agua de mi copa y devoras mi pan.

La puerta del suicida está abierta, pero los teólogos afirman que en la sombra ulterior del otro reino estaré yo, esperándome.

THE WATCHER

The light enters and I remember who I am; he is there.

He begins by telling me his name which (it should now be clear) is mine.

I revert to the servitude which has lasted more than seven times ten years.

He saddles me with his rememberings.

He saddles me with the miseries of every day, the human condition.

I am his old nurse; he requires me to wash his feet.

He spies on me in mirrors, in mahogany, in shop windows.

One or another woman has rejected him, and I must share his anguish.

He dictates to me now this poem, which I do not like.

He insists I apprentice myself tentatively to the stubborn Anglo-Saxon.

He has won me over to the hero worship of dead soldiers, people with whom I could scarcely exchange a single word.

On the last flight of stairs, I feel him at my side.

He is in my footsteps, in my voice.

Down to the last detail, I abhor him.

I am gratified to remark that he can hardly see.

I am in a circular cell and the infinite wall is closing in.

Neither of the two deceives the other, but we both lie.

We know each other too well, inseparable brother.

You drink the water from my cup and you wolf down my bread.

The door to suicide is open, but theologians assert that, in the subsequent shadows of the other kingdom, there will I be, waiting for myself.

AL IDIOMA ALEMÁN

Mi destino es la lengua castellana,
el bronce de Francisco de Quevedo,
pero en la lenta noche caminada
me exaltan otras músicas más íntimas.
Alguna me fue dada por la sangre—
oh voz de Shakespeare y de la Escritura—,
otras por el azar, que es dadivoso,
pero a ti, dulce lengua de Alemania,
te he elegido y buscado, solitario.
A través de vigilias y gramáticas,
de la jungla de las declinaciones,
del diccionario, que no acierta nunca
con el matiz preciso, fui acercándome.
Mis noches están llenas de Virgilio,
dije una vez; también pude haber dicho
de Hölderlin y de Angelus Silesius.
Heine me dio sus altos ruiseñores;
Goethe, la suerte de un amor tardío,
a la vez indulgente y mercenario;
Keller, la rosa que una mano deja
en la mano de un muerto que la amaba
y que nunca sabrá si es blanca o roja.
Tú, lengua de Alemania, eres tu obra
capital: el amor entrelazado
de las voces compuestas, las vocales
abiertas, los sonidos que permiten
el estudioso hexámetro del griego
y tu rumor de selvas y de noches.
Te tuve alguna vez. Hoy, en la linde
de los años cansados, te diviso
lejana como el álgebra y la luna.

TO THE GERMAN LANGUAGE

My destiny is in the Spanish language,
the bronze words of Francisco de Quevedo,
but in the long, slow progress of the night,
different, more intimate musics move me.
Some have been handed down to me by blood—
voices of Shakespeare, language of the Scriptures—
others by chance, which has been generous;
but you, gentle language of Germany,
I chose you, and I sought you out alone.
By way of grammar books and patient study,
through the thick undergrowth of the declensions,
the dictionary, which never puts its thumb on
the precise nuance, I kept moving closer.
My nights were full of overtones of Virgil,
I once said; but I could as well have named
Hölderlin, Angelus Silesius.
Heine lent me his lofty nightingales;
Goethe, the good fortune of late love,
at the same time both greedy and indulgent;
Keller, the rose which one hand leaves behind
in the closed fist of a dead man who adored it,
who will never know if it is white or red.
German language, you are your masterpiece:
love interwound in all your compound voices
and open vowels, sounds which accommodate
the studious hexameters of Greek
and undercurrents of jungles and of nights.
Once, I had you. Now, at the far extreme
of weary years, I feel you have become
as out of reach as algebra and the moon.

1891

Apenas lo entreveo y ya lo pierdo.
Ajustado el decente traje negro
y con una chalina como todas,
la frente angosta y el bigote ralo,
camina entre la gente de la tarde
ensimismado y sin mirar a nadie.
En una esquina de la calle Piedras
pide una caña brasilera. El hábito.
Alguien le grita adiós. No le contesta.
Hay en los ojos un rencor antiguo.
Otra cuadra. Una racha de milonga
le llega desde un patio. Esos changangos
están siempre amolando la paciencia,
pero al andar se hamaca y no lo sabe.
Sube la mano y palpa la firmeza
del puñal en la sisa del chaleco.
Va a cobrarse una deuda. Falta poco.
Unos pasos y el hombre se detiene.
En el zaguán hay una flor de cardo.
Oye el golpe del balde en el aljibe
y una voz que conoce demasiado.
Empuja la cancel que aún está abierta
como si lo esperaran. Esta noche
tal vez ya lo habrán muerto.

1891

I catch a glimpse of him and then I lose him—
best black suit well-brushed and narrow-fitting,
nondescript neckerchief around the throat,
narrow forehead, straggling moustache,
he walks among the people of the evening,
lost in himself, not seeing anyone.
At a corner counter on the Calle Piedras
he takes a shot of spirits, out of habit.
Someone calls out to him. He doesn't answer.
Behind his eyes, an old resentment smolders.
Another block. A fragment of milonga
falls from a patio. Those cheap guitars
keep gnawing at the edges of his temper,
but still, his walk keeps time, unconsciously.
He lifts his hand and pats the solid handle
of the dagger in the collar of his waistcoat.
He goes to reclaim a debt. It is not far.
A few steps, and the man stops in his walking.
In the passageway, there is a flowering thistle.
He hears the clunk of a bucket in the cistern
and a voice already too well-known to him.
He pushes the far door, which is already open
as though he were expected. This very evening
perhaps they will have shown him his own death.

MILONGA DE MANUEL FLORES

Manuel Flores va a morir.
Eso es moneda corriente;
morir es una costumbre
que sabe tener la gente.

Y sin embargo me duele
decirle adiós a la vida,
esa cosa tan de siempre,
tan dulce y tan conocida.

Miro en el alba mi mano,
miro en la mano las venas;
con extrañeza las miro
como si fueran ajenas.

Mañana vendrá la bala
y con la bala el olvido.
Lo dijo el sabio Merlín:
morir es haber nacido.

¡Cuánta cosa en su camino
Estos ojos habrán visto!
Quién sabe lo que verán
después que me juzgue Cristo.

Manuel Flores va a morir.
Eso es moneda corriente;
morir es una costumbre
que sabe tener la gente.

Manuel Flores is doomed to die.
That's as sure as your money.
Dying is a custom
well-known to many.

But even so, it pains me
to say goodbye to living,
that state so well-known now,
so sweet, so solid-seeming.

I look at my hand in the dawning.
I look at the veins contained there.
I look at them in amazement
as I would look at a stranger.

Tomorrow comes the bullet,
oblivion descending.
Merlin the magus said it:
being born has an ending.

So much these eyes have seen,
such things, such places!
Who knows what they will see
when I've been judged by Jesus.

Manuel Flores is doomed to die.
That's as sure as your money.
Dying is a custom
well-known to many.

EL SUEÑO DE PEDRO HENRÍQUEZ UREÑA

El sueño que Pedro Henríquez Ureña tuvo en el alba de uno de los días de 1946 curiosamente no constaba de imágenes sino de pausadas palabras. La voz que las decía no era la suya pero se parecía a la suya. El tono, pese a las posibilidades patéticas que el tema permitía, era impersonal y común. Durante el sueño, que fue breve, Pedro sabía que estaba durmiendo en su cuarto y que su mujer estaba a su lado. En la obscuridad el sueño le dijo:

Hará unas cuantas noches, en una esquina de la calle Córdoba, discutiste con Borges la invocación del Anónimo Sevillano *Oh Muerte, ven callada como sueles venir en la saeta*. Sospecharon que era el eco deliberado de algún texto latino, ya que esas traslaciones correspondían a los hábitos de una época, del todo ajena a nuestro concepto del plagio, sin duda menos literario que comercial. Lo que no sospecharon, lo que no podían sospechar, es que el diálogo era profético. Dentro de unas horas, te apresurarás por el último andén de Constitución, para dictar tu clase en la Universidad de La Plata. Alcanzarás el tren, pondrás la cartera en la red y te acomodarás en tu asiento, junto a la ventanilla. Alguien, cuyo nombre no sé pero cuya cara estoy viendo, te dirigirá unas palabras. No le contestarás, porque estarás muerto. Ya te habrás despedido como siempre de tu mujer y de tus hijas. No recordarás este sueño porque tu olvido es necesario para que se cumplan los hechos.

THE DREAM OF PEDRO HENRÍQUEZ UREÑA

The dream which Pedro Henríquez Ureña dreamed close to dawn one day in 1946 consisted, oddly enough, not of images but of slow, specific words. The voice which spoke them was not his own, but resembled it. Its tone, in spite of the mournful possibilities implicit in what it said, was impersonal and matter-of-fact. During the dream, which was short, Pedro knew that he was asleep in his own room, with his wife at his side. In the dark, the dream addressed him:

Some nights ago, on a corner of the Calle Córdoba, you discussed with Borges the invocation of the Anonymous One of Seville: "O Death come in silence as you are wont to do in the hands of the clock." You both suspected it to be the deliberate echo of some Latin text, inasmuch as these transliterations corresponded with the habits of a particular time, totally outside our own notions of plagiarism, unquestionably less literary than practical. What you did not suspect, what you could not suspect, is that the dialogue was a prophetic one. In a few hours, you will be hurrying along the last platform of Constitution Station, to give your class at the University of La Plata. You will catch the train, put your briefcase on the rack and settle in your seat, beside the window. Someone, whose name I do not know but whose face I am seeing, will address some words to you. You will not reply, because you will be dead. You will already have said goodbye, as usual, to your wife and children. You will not remember this dream, because your forgetting is necessary to the fulfillment of these events.

37

EL PALACIO

El Palacio no es infinito.

Los muros, los terraplenes, los jardines, los laberintos, las gradas, las terrazas, los antepechos, las puertas, las galerías, los patios circulares o rectangulares, los claustros, las encrucijadas, los aljibes, las antecámaras, las cámaras, las alcobas, las bibliotecas, los desvanes, las cárceles, las celdas sin salida y los hipogeos, no son menos cuantiosos que los granos de arena del Ganges, pero su cifra tiene un fin. Desde las azoteas, hacia el poniente, no falta quien divise las herrerías, las carpinterías, las caballerizas, los astilleros y las chozas de los esclavos.

A nadie le está dado recorrer más que una parte infinitesimal del palacio. Alguno no conoce sino los sótanos. Podemos percibir unas caras, unas voces, unas palabras, pero lo que percibimos es ínfimo. Ínfimo y precioso a la vez. La fecha que el acero graba en la lápida y que los libros parroquiales registran es posterior a nuestra muerte; ya estamos muertos cuando nada nos toca, ni una palabra, ni un anhelo, ni una memoria. Yo sé que no estoy muerto.

THE PALACE

The Palace is not infinite.

The walls, the ramparts, the gardens, the labyrinths, the staircases, the terraces, the parapets, the doors, the galleries, the circular or rectangular patios, the cloisters, the intersections, the cisterns, the anterooms, the chambers, the alcoves, the libraries, the attics, the dungeons, the sealed cells and the vaults, are not less in quantity than the grains of sand in the Ganges, but their number has a limit. From the roofs, toward sunset, many people can make out the forges, the workshops, the stables, the boatyards and the huts of the slaves.

It is granted to no one to traverse more than an infinitesimal part of the palace. Some know only the cellars. We can take in some faces, some voices, some words, but what we perceive is of the feeblest. Feeble and precious at the same time. The date which the chisel engraves in the tablet, and which is recorded in the parochial registers, is later than our own death; we are already dead when nothing touches us, neither a word nor a yearning nor a memory. I know that I am not dead.

Hengist quiere hombres.

Acudirán de los confines de arena que se pierden en largos mares, de chozas llenas de humo, de tierras pobres, de hondos bosques de lobos, en cuyo centro indefinido está el Mal.

Los labradores dejarán el arado y los pescadores las redes.

Dejarán sus mujeres y sus hijos, porque el hombre sabe que en cualquier lugar de la noche puede hallarlas y hacerlos.

Hengist el mercenario quiere hombres.

Los quiere para debelar una isla que todavía no se llama Inglaterra.

Lo seguirán sumisos y crueles.

Saben que siempre fue el primero en la batalla de hombres.

Saben que una vez olvidó su deber de venganza y que le dieron una espada desnuda y que la espada hizo su obra.

Atravesarán a remo los mares, sin brújula y sin mástil.

Traerán espadas y broqueles, yelmos con la forma del jabalí, conjuros para que se multipliquen las mieses, vagas cosmogonías, fábulas de los hunos y de los godos.

Conquistarán la tierra, pero nunca entrarán en las ciudades que Roma abandonó, porque son cosas demasiado complejas para su mente bárbara.

Hengist los quiere para la victoria, para el saqueo, para la corrupción de la carne y para el olvido.

Hengist los quiere (pero no lo sabe) para la fundación

Hengist wants men.

They will rally from the edges of sand which dissolve into broad seas, from huts filled with smoke, from thread-bare landscapes, from deep forests haunted by wolves, in whose vague center Evil lurks.

The ploughman will abandon the plough and the fisher-men their nets.

They will leave their wives and their children, for a man knows that anywhere in the night he can encounter the one and engender the other.

Hengist the mercenary wants men.

He wants them to subdue an island which is not yet called England.

Cowed and vicious, they will follow him.

They know him always to have been the first among men in battle.

They know that once he forgot his vow of vengeance and that they gave him a naked sword and that the sword did its work.

They will try their oars against the seas, with neither compass nor mast.

They will bear swords and bucklers, helmets in the like-ness of the boar's head, spells to make the cornfields multiply, vague cosmogonies, legends of the Huns and the Goths.

They will conquer the ground, but never will they enter the cities which Rome abandoned, for these are things too complicated for their primitive minds.

Hengist wants them for the victory, for the pillaging, for for the corruption of the flesh and for oblivion.

Hengist wants them (but he does not know it) for the

del mayor imperio, para que canten Shakespeare y Whitman, para que dominen el mar las naves de Nelson, para que Adán y Eva se alejen, tomados de la mano y silenciosos, del Paraíso que han perdido.

Hengist los quiere (pero no lo sabrá) para que yo trace estas letras.

founding of the greatest of empires, for the singing
of Shakespeare and Whitman, for Nelson's ships to
rule the sea, for Adam and Eve to be banished, hand
in hand and silent, from the Paradise they have lost.
Hengist wants them (but he cannot know it) so that I
may form these letters.

A UN GATO

No son más silenciosos los espejos
ni más furtiva el alba aventurera;
eres, bajo la luna, esa pantera
que nos es dado divisar de lejos.
Por obra indescifrable de un decreto
divino, te buscamos vanamente;
más remoto que el Ganges y el poniente,
tuya es la soledad, tuyo el secreto.
Tu lomo condesciende a la morosa
caricia de mi mano. Has admitido,
desde esa eternidad que ya es olvido,
el amor de la mano recelosa.
En otro tiempo estás. Eres el dueño
de un ámbito cerrado como un sueño.

TO A CAT

Mirrors are not more wrapt in silences
nor the arriving dawn more secretive;
you, in the moonlight, are that panther figure
which we can only spy at from a distance.
By the mysterious functioning of some
divine decree, we seek you out in vain;
remoter than the Ganges or the sunset,
yours is the solitude, yours is the secret.
Your back allows the tentative caress
my hand extends. And you have condescended,
since that forever, now oblivion,
to take love from a flattering human hand.
You live in other time, lord of your realm—
a world as closed and separate as dream.

EL ORO DE LOS TIGRES

Hasta la hora del ocaso amarillo
cuántas veces habré mirado
al poderoso tigre de Bengala
ir y venir por el predestinado camino
detrás de los barrotes de hierro,
sin sospechar que eran su cárcel.
Después vendrían otros tigres,
el tigre de fuego de Blake;
después vendrían otros oros,
el metal amoroso que era Zeus,
el anillo que cada nueve noches
engendra nueve anillos y éstos, nueve,
y no hay un fin.
Con los años fueron dejándome
los otros hermosos colores
y ahora sólo me quedan
la vaga luz, la inextricable sombra
y el oro del principio.
Oh ponientes, oh tigres, oh fulgores
del mito y de la épica,
oh un oro más precioso, tu cabello
que ansían estas manos.

THE GOLD OF THE TIGERS

Up to the moment of the yellow sunset,
how many times will I have cast my eyes on
the sinewy-bodied tiger of Bengal
toing and froing on its paced-out path
behind the labyrinthine iron bars,
never suspecting them to be a prison.
Afterward, other tigers will appear:
the blazing tiger of Blake, burning bright;
and after that will come the other golds—
the amorous gold shower disguising Zeus,
the gold ring which, on every ninth night,
gives light to nine rings more, and these, nine more,
and there is never an end.
All the other overwhelming colors,
in company with the years, kept leaving me,
and now alone remains
the amorphous light, the inextricable shadow
and the gold of the beginning.
O sunsets, O tigers, O wonders
of myth and epic,
O gold more dear to me, gold of your hair
which these hands crave to touch.

YO

La calavera, el corazón secreto,
los caminos de sangre que no veo,
los túneles del sueño, ese Proteo,
las vísceras, la nuca, el esqueleto.
Soy esas cosas. Increíblemente
soy también la memoria de una espada
y la de un solitario sol poniente
que se dispersa en oro, en sombra, en nada.
Soy él que ve las proas desde el puerto;
soy los contados libros, los contados
grabados por el tiempo fatigados;
soy él que envidia a los que ya se han muerto.
Más raro es ser el hombre que entrelaza
palabras en un cuarto de una casa.

I

The skull within, the secret, shuttered heart,
the byways of the blood I never see,
the underworld of dreaming, that Proteus,
the nape, the viscera, the skeleton.
I am all those things. Amazingly,
I am too the memory of a sword
and of a solitary, falling sun,
turning itself to gold, then gray, then nothing.
I am the one who sees the approaching ships
from harbor. And I am the dwindled books,
the rare engravings worn away by time;
the one who envies those already dead.
Stranger to be the man who interlaces
such words as these, in some room, in a house.

EL SUEÑO

Cuando los relojes de la media noche prodiguen
un tiempo generoso,
iré más lejos que los bogavantes de Ulises
a la región del sueño, inaccesible
a la memoria humana.
De esa región inmersa rescato restos
que no acabo de comprender:
hierbas de sencilla botánica,
animales algo diversos,
diálogos con los muertos,
Rostros que realmente son máscaras,
palabras de lenguajes muy antiguos
y a veces un horror incomparable
al que nos puede dar el día.
Seré todos o nadie. Seré el otro
que sin saberlo soy, él que ha mirado
ese otro sueño, mi vigilia. La juzga,
resignado y sonriente.

THE DREAM

While the clocks of the midnight hours are squandering
an abundance of time,
I shall go, farther than the shipmates of Ulysses,
to the territory of dream, beyond the reach
of human memory.
From that underwater world I save some fragments,
inexhaustible to my understanding:
grasses from some primitive botany,
animals of all kinds,
conversations with the dead,
faces which all the time are masks,
words out of very ancient languages,
and at times, horror, unlike anything
the day can offer us.
I shall be all or no one. I shall be the other
I am without knowing it, he who has looked on
that other dream, my waking state. He weighs it up,
resigned and smiling.

BROWNING RESUELVE SER POETA

Por estos rojos laberintos de Londres
descubro que he elegido
la más curiosa de las profesiones humanas,
salvo que todas, a su modo, lo son.
Como los alquimistas
que buscaron la piedra filosofal
en el azogue fugitivo,
haré que las comunes palabras—
naipes marcados del tahur, moneda de la plebe—
rindan la magia que fue suya
cuando Thor era el numen y el estrépito,
el trueno y la plegaria.
En el dialecto de hoy
diré a mi vez las cosas eternas;
trataré de no ser indigno
del gran eco de Byron.
Este polvo que soy será invulnerable.
Si una mujer comparte mi amor
mi verso rozará la décima esfera de los cielos concéntricos;
si una mujer desdeña mi amor
haré de mi tristeza una música,
un alto río que siga resonando en el tiempo.
Viviré de olvidarme.
Seré la cara que entreveo y que olvido,
seré Judas que acepta
la divina misión de ser traidor,
seré Calibán en la ciénaga,
seré un soldado mercenario que muere
sin temor y sin fe,
seré Polícrates que ve con espanto
el anillo devuelto por el destino,
seré el amigo que me odia.

BROWNING RESOLVES TO BE A POET

In these red London labyrinths
I find that I have chosen
the most curious of human professions,
though given that all are curious, in their way.
Like alchemists
who looked for the philosopher's stone
in elusive quicksilver,
I shall make ordinary words—
the marked cards of the sharper, the people's coinage—
yield up the magic which was theirs
when Thor was inspiration and eruption,
thunder and worship.
In the wording of the day,
I in my turn will say eternal things;
I will try to be not unworthy
of the great echo of Byron.
This dust that is me will be invulnerable.
If a woman partakes of my love,
my poem will graze the tenth sphere of the concentric heavens;
if a woman shrugs off my love,
I will make music out of my misery,
a vast river reverberating on through time.
I will live by forgetting myself.
I will be the face I half-see and forget,
I will be Judas who accepts
the blessed destiny of being a traitor,
I will be Caliban in the swamp,
I will be a mercenary dying
without fear or faith,
I will be Polycrates, horrified to see
the ring returned by destiny,
I will be the friend who hates me.

El persa me dará el ruiseñor y Roma la espada.
Máscaras, agonías, resurrecciones,
destejerán y tejerán mi suerte
y alguna vez seré Robert Browning.

Persia will grant me the nightingale, Rome the sword.
Agonies, masks and resurrections
will weave and unweave my fate
and at some point I will be Robert Browning.

INVENTARIO

Hay que arrimar una escalera para subir. Un tramo le falta.
¿Qué podemos buscar en el altillo
sino lo que amontona el desorden?
Hay olor a humedad.
El atardecer entra por la pieza de plancha.
Las vigas del cielo raso están cerca y el piso está vencido.
Nadie se atreve a poner el pie.
Hay un catre de tijera desvencijado.
Hay unas herramientas inútiles.
Está el sillón de ruedas del muerto.
Hay un pie de lámpara.
Hay una hamaca paraguaya con borlas, deshilachada.
Hay aparejos y papeles.
Hay una lámina del estado mayor de Aparicio Saravia.
Hay una vieja plancha a carbón.
Hay un reloj de tiempo detenido, con el péndulo roto.
Hay un marco desdorado, sin tela.
Hay un tablero de cartón y unas piezas descabaladas.
Hay un brasero de dos patas.
Hay una petaca de cuero.
Hay un ejemplar enmohecido del *Libro de los Mártires* de
    Foxe, en intrincada letra gótica.
Hay una fotografía que ya puede ser de cualquiera.
Hay una piel gastada que fue de tigre.
Hay una llave que ha perdido su puerta.
¿Qué podemos buscar en el altillo
sino lo que amontona el desorden?
Al olvido, a las cosas del olvido, acabo de erigir este monu-
    mento,
sin duda menos perdurable que el bronce y que se confunde
    con ellas.

INVENTORY

To reach it, a ladder has to be set up. There is no stair.
What can we be looking for in the attic
but the accumulation of disorder?
There is a smell of damp.
The late afternoon enters by way of the laundry.
The ceiling beams loom close, and the floor has rotted.
Nobody dares to put a foot on it.
A folding cot, broken.
A few useless tools,
the dead one's wheelchair.
The base for a lamp.
A Paraguayan hammock with tassels, all frayed away.
Equipment and papers.
An engraving of Aparacio Savaria's general staff.
An old charcoal iron.
A clock stopped in time, with a broken pendulum.
A peeling gilt frame, with no canvas.
A cardboard chessboard, and some broken chessmen.
A stove with only two legs.
A chest made of leather.
A mildewed copy of Foxe's *Book of Martyrs,* in intricate
    Gothic lettering.
A photograph which might be of anybody.
A worn skin, once a tiger's.
A key which has lost its lock.
What can we be looking for in the attic
except the flotsam of disorder?
To forgetting, to all forgotten objects, I have just erected this
    monument
(unquestionably less durable than bronze) which will be lost
    among them.

EL SUICIDA

No quedará en la noche una estrella.
No quedará la noche.
Moriré y conmigo la suma
del intolerable universo.
Borraré las pirámides, las medallas,
los continentes y las caras.
Borraré la acumulación del pasado.
Haré polvo la historia, polvo el polvo.
Estoy mirando el último poniente.
Oigo el último pájaro.
Lego la nada a nadie.

THE SUICIDE

Not a single star will be left in the night.
The night will not be left.
I will die and, with me,
the weight of the intolerable universe.
I shall erase the pyramids, the medallions,
the continents and faces.
I shall erase the accumulated past.
I shall make dust of history, dust of dust.
Now I am looking on the final sunset.
I am hearing the last bird.
I bequeath nothingness to no one.

AL RUISEÑOR

¿En qué noche secreta de Inglaterra
o del constante Rhin incalculable,
perdida entre las noches de mis noches,
a mi ignorante oído habrá llegado
tu voz cargada de mitologías,
ruiseñor de Virgilio y de los persas?
Quizá nunca te oí, pero a mi vida
se une tu vida, inseparablemente.
Un espíritu errante fue tu símbolo
en un libro de enigmas. El Marino
te apodaba sirena de los bosques
y cantas en la noche de Julieta
y en la intrincada página latina
y desde los pinares de aquel otro
ruiseñor de Judea y de Alemania,
Heine el burlón, el encendido, el triste.
Keats te oyó para todos, para siempre.
No habrá uno solo entre los claros nombres
que los pueblos te dan sobre la tierra
que no quiera ser digno de tu música,
ruiseñor de la sombra. El agareno
te soñó arrebatado por el éxtasis
el pecho traspasado por la espina
de la cantada rosa que enrojeces
con tu sangre final. Asiduamente
urdo en la hueca tarde este ejercicio,
ruiseñor de la arena y de los mares,
que en la memoria, exaltación y fábula,
ardes de amor y mueres melodioso.

TO THE NIGHTINGALE

Out of what secret English summer evening
or night on the incalculable Rhine,
lost among all the nights of my long night,
could it have come to my unknowing ear,
your song, encrusted with mythology,
nightingale of Virgil and the Persians?
Perhaps I never heard you, but my life
is bound up with your life, inseparably.
The symbol for you was a wandering spirit
in a book of enigmas. And among all sailors,
you were nicknamed "siren of the woods";
you sing throughout the night of Juliet
and through the intricate pages of the Latin
and from the pinewoods of that other one,
the nightingale of Germany and Judea,
Heine, the clown, the man on fire, the sad one.
Keats heard your song for everyone, for ever.
There is not one among the shimmering names
people have given you across the earth
which does not seek to match your own music,
nightingale of the dark. The Muslim dreamed you
in the delirium of ecstasy,
his breast pierced by the thorn of the sung rose
you redden with your blood. Assiduously
in the black evening I contrive this poem,
nightingale of the sands and all the seas,
that in exultation, memory and fable,
you burn with love and die in liquid song.

SOY

Soy él que sabe que no es menos vano
que el vano observador que en el espejo
de silencio y cristal sigue el reflejo
o el cuerpo (da lo mismo) del hermano.
Soy, tácitos amigos, él que sabe
que no hay otra venganza que el olvido
ni otro perdón. Un dios ha concedido
al odio humano esta curiosa llave.
Soy él que pese a tan ilustres modos
de errar, no ha descifrado el laberinto
singular y plural, arduo y distinto,
del tiempo, que es de uno y es de todos.
Soy él que es nadie, él que no fue una espada
en la guerra. Soy eco, olvido, nada.

I AM

I am he who knows himself no less vain
than the vain looker-on who in the mirror
of glass and silence follows the reflection
or body (it's the same thing) of his brother.
I am, my silent friends, the one who knows
there is no other pardon or revenge
than sheer oblivion. A god has granted
this odd solution to all human hates.
Despite my many wondrous wanderings,
I am the one who never has unraveled
the labyrinth of time, singular, plural,
grueling, strange, one's own and everyone's.
I am no one. I did not wield a sword
in battle. I am echo, emptiness, nothing.

QUINCE MONEDAS

A Alicia Jurado

UN POETA ORIENTAL

Durante cien otoños he mirado
tu tenue disco.
Durante cien otoños he mirado
tu arco sobre las islas.
Durante cien otoños mis labios
no han sido menos silenciosos.

EL DESIERTO

El espacio sin tiempo.
La luna es del color de la arena.
Ahora, precisamente ahora,
mueren los hombres del Metauro y de Trafalgar.

LLUEVE

¿En qué ayer, en qué patios de Cartago,
cae también esta lluvia?

ASTERIÓN

El año me tributa mi pasto de hombres
y en la cisterna hay agua.
En mí se anudan los caminos de piedra.
¿De qué puedo quejarme?
En los atardeceres
me pesa un poco la cabeza de toro.

UN POETA MENOR

La meta es el olvido.
Yo he llegado antes.

FIFTEEN COINS

To Alicia Jurado

AN ORIENTAL POET

A hundred autumns I have looked upon
your uncertain disc.
A hundred autumns I have looked upon
your rainbow over the islands.
A hundred autumns and my lips
have never been less silent.

THE DESERT

Space without time.
The moon is the same color as the sand.
Now, at this precise hour,
the men of Metaurus and Trafalgar die.

IT IS RAINING

In what yesterday, in what patios of Carthage,
does this rain also fall?

ASTERION

The year awards to me my human fodder
and in the cisterns there is water.
In me, the stony paths crisscross.
What can I complain of?
In the late afternoons,
the bull's head weighs on me a little.

A MINOR POET

The goal is oblivion.
I have arrived early.

GÉNESIS, IV, 8

Fue en el primer desierto.
Dos brazos arrojaron una gran piedra.
No hubo un grito. Hubo sangre.
Hubo por vez primera la muerte.
Ya no recuerdo si fui Abel o Caín.

NORTUMBRIA, A.D. 900

Que antes del alba lo despojen los lobos;
la espada es el camino más corto.

MIGUEL DE CERVANTES

Crueles estrellas y propicias estrellas
presidieron la noche de mi génesis;
debo a las últimas la cárcel
en que soñé Quijote.

EL OESTE

El callejón final con su poniente.
Inauguración de la pampa.
Inauguración de la muerte.

ESTANCIA EL RETIRO

El tiempo juega un ajedrez sin piezas
en el patio. El crujido de una rama
rasga la noche. Fuera la llanura
leguas de polvo y sueño desparrama.
Sombras los dos, copiamos lo que dictan
otras sombras: Heráclito y Gautama.

EL PRISIONERO

Una lima.
La primera de las pesadas puertas de hierro.
Algún día seré libre.

GENESIS IV, 8

It was in the original desert.
Two arms let loose a great stone.
There was no cry. There was blood.
For the first time there was death.
I do not recall now if I was Abel or Cain.

NORTHUMBRIA, A.D. 900

Let the wolves savage him before dawn;
the sword is the quickest way.

MIGUEL DE CERVANTES

Both cruel stars and propitious stars
watched over the evening of my genesis;
to the last of those I owe the prison
in which I dreamed of Don Quixote.

THE WEST

The final alley with its setting sun.
Beginning of the pampa.
Beginning of death.

THE RETIRO RANCH

Time plays a game of chess without the pieces
in the patio. The creaking of a branch
gnaws away at the night. Outside, the plain
squanders its endless leagues of dust and dream.
Both of us shadows, we copy out the dictates
of other shadows: Guatama, Heraclitus.

THE PRISONER

A file.
The first of the solid iron doors.
One day I will be free.

MACBETH

Nuestros actos prosiguen su camino,
que no conoce término.
Maté a mi rey para que Shakespeare
urdiera su tragedia.

ETERNIDADES

La serpiente que ciñe el mar y es el mar,
el repetido remo de Jasón, la joven espada de Sigurd.
Sólo perduran en el tiempo las cosas
que no fueron del tiempo.

EDGAR ALLEN POE

Los sueños que he soñado. El pozo y el péndulo.
El hombre de las multitudes. Ligeia . . .
Pero también este otro.

EL ESPÍA

En la pública luz de las batallas
otros dan su vida a la patria
Y los recuerda el mármol.
Yo he errado oscuro por ciudades que odio.
Le di otras cosas.
Abjuré de mi honor,
traicioné a quienes me creyeron su amigo,
compré conciencias,
abominé del nombre de la patria,
me resigné a la infamia.

MACBETH

Our acts continue on their destined way
which does not know an end.
I slew my sovereign so that Shakespeare
might plot his tragedy.

ETERNITIES

The serpent which circles the sea and is the sea,
the recurring oar of Jason, the young sword of Sigurd.
In time, only those things last
which have not been in time.

EDGAR ALLEN POE

The dreams that I have dreamed. The pit and the pendulum.
The man of the multitudes. Ligeia . . .
But also this other one.

THE SPY

In the public glare of battles
others give their lives for their country
and are remembered in marble.
I gave it other things.
I foreswore my honor,
I betrayed those who believed me their friend,
I purchased consciences,
I abominated the name of my country,
I gave myself up to infamy.

PROTEO

Antes que los remeros de Odiseo
fatigaran el mar color de vino
las inasibles formas adivino
de aquel dios cuyo nombre fue Proteo.
Pastor de los rebaños de los mares
y poseedor del don de profecía,
prefería ocultar lo que sabía
y entretejer oráculos dispares.
Urgido por las gentes asumía
la forma de un león o de una hoguera
o de árbol que da sombra a la ribera
o de agua que en el agua se perdía.
De Proteo el egipcio no te asombres,
tú, que eres uno y eres muchos hombres.

PROExpandedForm PROTEUS

Before the oarsmen of Odysseus
were able to exhaust the wine-dark sea,
I can divine the indefinable forms
of that old god whose name was Proteus.
Shepherd of the wave-flocks of the waters
and wielder of the gift of prophecy,
he liked to make a secret of his knowledge
and weave a pattern of ambiguous answers.
At the demand of people, he took on
the substance of a lion or a bonfire
or a tree, spreading shade on the river bank
or water which would disappear in water.
Do not take fright at Proteus the Egyptian,
you, who are one, and also many men.

Nadie a tu lado.
Anoche maté a un hombre en la batalla.
Era animoso y alto, de la clara estirpe de Anlaf.
La espada entró en el pecho, un poco a la izquierda.
Rodó por tierra y fue una cosa,
una cosa del cuervo.
En vano lo esperarás, mujer que no he visto.
No lo traerán las naves que huyeron
sobre el agua amarilla.
En la hora del alba,
tu mano desde el sueño lo buscará.
Tu lecho está frío.
Anoche maté a un hombre en Brunanburh.

No one at your side.
Last night I did a man to death in battle.
He was spirited and tall, of the clear line of Anlaf.
The sword went into his breast, a shade to the left.
He turned on the ground and was a thing,
an object for crows.
In vain will you await him, wife I have not seen.
They will not bear him back, the ships that fled
over the yellow waters.
In the hour of the dawn,
out of a dream, your hand will reach for him.
Your couch is cold.
Last night I killed a man in Brunanburh.

EL CIEGO

Lo han despojado del diverso mundo,
de los rostros, que son lo que eran antes,
de las cercanas calles, hoy distantes,
y del cóncavo azul, ayer profundo.
De los libros le queda lo que deja
la memoria, esa forma del olvido
que retiene el formato, no el sentido,
y que los meros títulos refleja.
El desnivel acecha. Cada paso
puede ser la caída. Soy el lento
prisionero de un tiempo soñoliento
que no marca su aurora ni su ocaso.
Es de noche. No hay otros. Con el verso
debo labrar mi insípido universo.

II

Desde mi nacimiento, que fue el noventa y nueve
de la cóncava parra y el aljibe profundo,
el tiempo minucioso, que en la memoria es breve,
me fue hurtando las formas visibles de este mundo.
Los días y las noches limaron los perfiles
de las letras humanas y los rostros amados;
en vano interrogaron mis ojos agotados
las vanas bibliotecas y los vanos atriles.
El azul y el bermejo son ahora una niebla
y dos voces inútiles. El espejo que miro
es una cosa gris. En el jardín aspiro,
amigos, una lóbrega rosa de la tiniebla.
Ahora sólo perduran las formas amarillas
y sólo puedo ver para ver pesadillas.

THE BLIND MAN

I

He is divested of the diverse world,
of faces, which still stay as once they were,
of the adjoining streets, now far away,
and of the concave sky, once infinite.
Of books, he keeps no more than what is left him
by memory, that brother of forgetting,
which keeps the formula but not the feeling
and which reflects no more than tag and name.
Traps lie in wait for me. My every step
might be a fall. I am a prisoner
shuffling through a time which feels like dream,
taking no note of mornings or of sunsets.
It is night. I am alone. In verse like this,
I must create my insipid universe.

II

Since I was born, in 1899,
beside the concave vine and the deep cistern,
frittering time, so brief in memory,
kept taking from me all my eye-shaped world.
Both days and nights would wear away the profiles
of human letters and of well-loved faces.
My wasted eyes would ask their useless questions
of pointless libraries and lecterns.
Blue and vermilion both are now a fog,
both useless sounds. The mirror I look into
is gray. I breathe a rose across the garden,
a wistful rose, my friends, out of the twilight.
Only the shades of yellow stay with me
and I can see only to look on nightmares.

UN CIEGO

No sé cuál es la cara que me mira
cuando miro la cara del espejo;
no sé qué anciano acecha en su reflejo
con silenciosa y ya cansada ira.
Lento en mi sombra, con la mano exploro
mis invisibles rasgos. Un destello
me alcanza. He vislumbrado tu cabello
que es de ceniza o es aún de oro.
Repito que he perdido solamente
la vana superficie de las cosas.
El consuelo es de Milton y es valiente,
pero pienso en las letras y en las rosas.
Pienso que si pudiera ver mi cara
sabría quién soy en esta tarde rara.

A BLIND MAN

I do not know what face is looking back
whenever I look at the face in the mirror;
I do not know what old face seeks its image
in silent and already weary anger.
Slow in my blindness, with my hand I feel
the contours of my face. A flash of light
gets through to me. I have made out your hair,
color of ash and at the same time, gold.
I say again that I have lost no more
than the inconsequential skin of things.
These wise words come from Milton, and are noble,
but then I think of letters and of roses.
I think, too, that if I could see my features,
I would know who I am, this precious afternoon.

Temí que el porvenir (que ya declina)
sería un profundo corredor de espejos
indistintos, ociosos y menguantes,
una repetición de vanidades,
y en la penumbra que precede al sueño
rogué a mis dioses, cuyo nombre ignoro,
que enviaran algo o alguien a mis días.
Lo hicieron. Es la Patria. Mis mayores
la sirvieron con largas proscripciones,
con penurias, con hambre, con batallas,
aquí de nuevo está el hermoso riesgo.
No soy aquellas sombras tutelares
que honré con versos que no olvida el tiempo.
Estoy ciego. He cumplido los setenta;
no soy el oriental Francisco Borges
que murió con dos balas en el pecho,
entre las agonías de los hombres,
en el hedor de un hospital de sangre,
pero la Patria, hoy profanada quiere
que con mi oscura pluma de gramático,
docta en las nimiedades académicas
y ajena a los trabajos de la espada,
congregue el gran rumor de la epopeya
y exija mi lugar. Lo estoy haciendo.

1972

I feared that the future, now already dwindling,
would be an extending corridor of mirrors,
useless and vague, their images on the wane,
a repetition of all vanities,
and in the half-light which precedes the dream,
I begged my gods, whose names I do not know,
to send something or someone into my days.
They did. It is my country. My own forebears
gave themselves up to it through long proscriptions,
in penury, in hunger, and in battle.
Here, once again, comes the alluring challenge.
I am not with those tutelary figures
I praised in verses still alive in time.
I am blind, and I have lived out seventy years.
I am not Francisco Borges from the east
who died with a brace of bullets in his breast
among the final agonies of men
in the death-stench of a hospital of blood;
but my country, violated now, insists
that with my tentative grammarian's pen,
well-schooled in academic tinkerings,
far from the warlike business of the sword,
I assemble the great rumble of the epic
and carve out my own place. I am doing it.

ELEGÍA

Tres muy antiguas caras me desvelan:
una el Océano, que habló con Claudio,
otra el Norte de aceros ignorantes
y atroces en la aurora y el ocaso,
la tercera la muerte, ese otro nombre
del incesante tiempo que nos roe.
La carga secular de los ayeres
de la historia que fue o que fue soñada
me abruma, personal como una culpa.
Pienso en la nave ufana que devuelve
a los mares el cuerpo de Scyld Sceaving
que reinó en Dinamarca bajo el cielo;
pienso en el alto lobo, cuyas riendas
eran sierpes, que dio al barco incendiado
la blancura del dios hermoso y muerto;
pienso en piratas cuya carne humana
es dispersión y limo bajo el peso
de los mares que fueron su aventura;
pienso en las tumbas que los navegantes
vieron desde boreales Odiseas.
Pienso en mi propia, en mi perfecta muerte,
sin la urna cineraria y sin la lágrima.

ELEGY

Three very ancient faces stay with me:
one is the Ocean, which would talk with Claudius,
another the North, with its unfeeling temper,
savage both at sunrise and at sunset;
the third is Death, that other name we give
to passing time, which wears us all away.
The secular burden of those yesterdays
from history which happened or was dreamed,
oppresses me as personally as guilt.
I think of the proud ship, carrying back
to sea the body of Scyld Sceaving,
who ruled in Denmark underneath the sky;
I think of the great wolf, whose reins were serpents,
who lent the burning boat the purity
and whiteness of the beautiful dead god;
I think of pirates too, whose human flesh
is scattered through the slime beneath the weight
of waters which were ground for their adventures;
I think of mausoleums which the sailors
saw in the course of Northern odyssies.
I think of my own death, my perfect death,
without a funeral urn, without a tear.

EL DESTERRADO (1977)

Alguien recorre los senderos de Itaca
y no se acuerda de su rey, que fue a Troya
hace ya tantos años;
alguien piensa en las tierras heredadas
y en el arado nuevo y el hijo
y es acaso feliz.
En el confín del orbe yo, Ulises,
descendí a la Casa de Hades
y vi la sombra del tebano Tiresias
que desligó el amor de las serpientes
y la sombra de Heracles
que mata sombras de leones en la pradera
y asimismo está en el Olimpo.
Alguien hoy anda por Bolívar y Chile
y puede ser feliz o no serlo.
Quién me diera ser él.

THE EXILE (1977)

Someone makes tracks along the paths of Ithaca
and has forgotten his king, who was at Troy
so many years ago;
someone is thinking of his new-won lands,
his new plough and his son,
and is happy, in the main.
Within the confines of the globe, myself, Ulysses,
descended deep into the Hall of Hades
and saw the shade of Tiresius of Thebes
who unlocked the love of the serpents
and the shade of Hercules
who kills the shades of lions on the plain
and at the same time occupies Olympus.
Someone today walks streets—Chile, Bolívar—
perhaps happy, perhaps not.
I wish I could be he.

EN MEMORIA DE ANGELICA

¡Cuántas posibles vidas se habrán ido
en esta pobre y diminuta muerte,
cuántas posibles vidas que la suerte
daría a la memoria o al olvido!
Cuando yo muera morirá un pasado;
con esta flor un porvenir ha muerto
en las aguas que ignoran, un abierto
porvenir por los astros arrasado.
Yo, como ella, muero de infinitos
destinos que el azar no me depara;
busca mi sombra los gastados mitos
de una patria que siempre dio la cara.
Un breve mármol cuida su memoria;
sobre nosotros crece, atroz, la historia.

IN MEMORY OF ANGELICA

How many possible lives must have gone out
in this so modest and diminutive death,
how many possible lives, which fate would turn
to memory, or else oblivion?
When I die too, a certain past will die;
with this small bloom, a yet-to-be has died
in the unfeeling water, a white future
blindly obliterated by the stars.
Like her, I am dead to infinite destinies
which chance makes inaccessible to me.
My shadow seeks out all the lifeless myths
within my country, which was always brave.
A slab of marble tends her memory.
Over us looms atrocious history.

MIS LIBROS

Mis libros (que no saben que yo existo)
son tan parte de mí como este rostro
de sienes grises y de grises ojos
que vanamente busco en los cristales
y que recorro con la mano cóncava.
No sin alguna lógica amargura
pienso que las palabras esenciales
que me expresan están en esas hojas
que no saben quién soy, no en las que he escrito.
Mejor así. Las voces de los muertos
me dirán para siempre.

MY BOOKS

My books (which do not know that I exist)
are as much part of me as is this face,
the temples gone to gray and the eyes gray,
the face I vainly look for in the mirror,
tracing its outline with a concave hand.
Not without understandable bitterness,
I feel now that the quintessential words
expressing me are in those very pages
which do not know me, not in those I have written.
It is better so. The voices of the dead
will speak to me for ever.

TALISMANES

Un ejemplar de la primera edición de la *Edda Islandorum* de Snorri, impresa en Dinamarca.

Los cinco tomos de la obra de Schopenhauer.

Los dos tomos de las *Odiseas* de Chapman.

Una espada que guerreó en el desierto.

Un mate con un pie de serpientes que mi bisabuelo trajo de Lima.

Un prisma de cristal.

Unos daguerrotipos borrosos.

Un globo terráqueo de madera que me dio Cecilia Ingenieros y que fue de su padre.

Un bastón de puño encorvado que anduvo por las llanuras de América, por Colombia y por Texas.

Varios cilindros de metal con diplomas.

La toga y el birrete de un doctorado.

Las Empresas de Saavedra Fajardo, en olorosa pasta española.

La memoria de una mañana.

Líneas de Virgilio y de Frost.

La voz de Macedonio Fernández.

El amor o el diálogo de unos pocos.

Ciertamente son talismanes, pero de nada sirven contra la sombra que no puedo nombrar, contra la sombra que no debo nombrar.

TALISMANS

A copy of the first edition of the *Edda Islandorum*, by Snorri,
   printed in Denmark.
The five volumes of the work of Schopenhauer.
The two volumes of Chapman's *Odyssey*.
A sword which fought in the desert.
A maté gourd with serpent feet which my great-grandfather
   brought from Lima.
A crystal prism.
A few eroded daguerrotypes.
A terraqueous wooden globe which Cecilia Ingenieros gave
   me and which belonged to her father.
A stick with a curved handle with which I walked on the
   plains of America, in Colombia and in Texas.
Various metal cylinders with diplomas.
The gown and mortarboard of a doctorate.
Las Empresas, by Saavedra Fajardo, bound in good-smelling
   Spanish board.
The memory of a morning.
Lines of Virgil and Frost.
The voice of Macedonio Fernandez.
The love or the conversation of a few people.
Certainly they are talismans, but useless against the dark
   I cannot name, the dark I must not name.

LA CIERVA BLANCA

¿De qué agreste balada de la verde Inglaterra,
de qué lámina persa, de qué región arcana
de las noches y días que nuestro ayer encierra,
vino la cierva blanca que soñé esta mañana?
Duraría un segundo. La vi cruzar el prado
y perderse en el oro de una tarde ilusoria,
leve criatura hecha de un poco de memoria
y de un poco de olvido, cierva de un solo lado.
Los númenes que rigen este curioso mundo
me dejaron soñarte pero no ser tu dueño;
tal vez en un recodo del porvenir profundo
te encontraré de nuevo, cierva blanca de un sueño.
Yo también soy un sueño fugitivo que dura
unos días más que el sueño del prado y la blancura.

THE WHITE DEER

Out of what country ballad of green England,
or Persian etching, out of what secret region
of nights and days enclosed in our lost past
came the white deer I dreamed of in the dawn?
A moment's flash. I saw it cross the meadow
and vanish in the golden afternoon,
a lithe, illusory creature, half-remembered
and half-imagined, deer with a single side.
The presences which rule this curious world
have let me dream of you but not command you.
Perhaps in a recess of the unplumbed future,
again I will find you, white deer from my dream.
I too am dream, lasting a few days longer
than that bright dream of whiteness and green fields.

LA ROSA PROFUNDA

A Susana Bombal

A los quinientos años de la Héjira
Persia miró desde sus alminares
la invasión de las lanzas del desierto
y Attar de Nishapur miró una rosa
y le dijo con tácita palabra
como él que piensa, no como él que reza:
—Tu vaga esfera está en mi mano. El tiempo
Nos encorva a los dos y nos ignora
en esta tarde de un jardín perdido.
Tu leve peso es húmedo en el aire.
La incesante pleamar de tu fragancia
sube a mi vieja cara que declina
pero te sé más lejos que aquel niño
que te entrevió en las láminas de un sueño
o aquí en este jardín, una mañana.
La blancura del sol puede ser tuya
o el oro de la luna o la bermeja
firmeza de la espada en la victoria.
Soy ciego y nada sé, pero preveo
que son más los caminos. Cada cosa
es infinitas cosas. Eres música,
firmamentos, palacios, ríos, ángeles,
rosa profunda, ilimitada, íntima,
que el Señor mostrará a mis ojos muertos.

THE UNENDING ROSE

To Susana Bombal

Five hundred years in the wake of the Hegira,
Persia looked down from its minarets
on the invasion of the desert lances,
and Attar of Nishapur gazed on a rose,
addressing it in words which had no sound,
as one who thinks rather than one who prays:
"Your fragile globe is in my hand; and time
is bending both of us, both unaware,
this afternoon, in a forgotten garden.
Your brittle shape is humid in the air.
The steady, tidal fullness of your fragrance
rises up to my old, declining face.
But I know you far longer than that child
who glimpsed you in the layers of a dream
or here, in this garden, once upon a morning.
The whiteness of the sun may well be yours
or the moon's gold, or else the crimson stain
on the hard sword-edge in the victory.
I am blind and I know nothing, but I see
there are more ways to go; and everything
is an infinity of things. You, you are music,
rivers, firmaments, palaces and angels,
O endless rose, intimate, without limit,
which the Lord will finally show to my dead eyes."

NOTES

"Tankas." I have attempted to adapt to our prosody the Japanese form that consists of a first line of five syllables, then one of seven, one of five, and the last two of seven. Who knows how these exercises sound to an Oriental ear. The original form also ignores rhyme.

"The Gold of the Tigers." For the ring of nine nights, the curious reader can look up chapter 49 of the Lesser Edda. The name of the ring was Draupnir.

"In Memory of Angelica." Borges's niece was drowned in a swimming pool at the age of six.